The Jewel of Friendship

The Jewel of Friendship

A Jataka Tale

Illustrated by Magdalena Duran

DHARMA PUBLISHING

First published 2002

Second edition 2009, augmented with guidance
for parents and teachers

Printed on acid-free paper

Printed in the United States of America by Dharma Press
35788 Hauser Bridge Road, Cazadero, California 95421

9   8   7   6   5   4   3   2

Library of Congress Cataloging-in-Publication Data

Jewel of Friendship

(Jataka Tales Series)
Summary: When a boy befriends a naga, a serpent-king in human form,
he understands that friendship is more precious than the rarest of jewels.

1.Jataka stories, English. [1. Jataka stories]
I. Duran, Magdalena, ill.   II. Series
BQ1462.E5 P54 2002   294.3'82325—dc21   00-060136

ISBN 978-0-89800-428-1

Dedicated to children everywhere

Once upon a time, in the far-off land of India in the great city of Benares, a good and generous teacher lived in the king's palace. The teacher had two sons he loved dearly. When the boys were barely out of school, their parents passed away and the two brothers had to leave the palace.

With great sadness, the brothers gathered every-thing they owned and left the city. Lost in grief, they wandered alone for several months until they came to a beautiful spot by the river Ganges where they decided to stay. Each boy built himself a small hut out of twigs, branches, and leaves. The older brother made his hut high up on the river bank, while the younger brother chose a cool spot lower down on the bank, close to the river's edge.

This peaceful place just happened to be home to a naga, a giant serpent-king who lived in a palace deep under the water and often surfaced to sunbath on the river's sunny banks. One day, soon after the brothers had settled in, the serpent-king passed by the younger brother's hut. Seeing that the youth was living there all by himself, he thought, "What a noble and brave young man! Maybe we could be friends."

The naga did not want to frighten the younger brother by appearing before him in his snake like form. Therefore he cast a magic spell that changed him into a young man of about the same age. The serpent-king approached the grieving boy and asked why he had chosen to live like a hermit in this beautiful but remote and lonely place.

The younger brother was happy with the company of someone so like himself and they talked for hours. Each day the serpent-king came to visit him and as time went by, the two young men became very close friends.

One day the serpent-king thought, "Maybe now that my friend knows me, he will accept me as I am and not be afraid when he sees that I am really a naga. I am sure he will still like me as before." So that day, just before returning to his palace, the naga lifted the spell and allowed the younger brother to see his true form.

What a tall and majestic creature he was! On his forehead rested the famous jewel that adorns all serpent-kings. It glowed like the iridescent feathers on a peacock's neck, shining out of the midnight blue crown of the serpent's head. Just like the sun at daybreak, the jewel sent out rays of light—soft orange, rosy pink, and buttery yellow streams that blended together in radiant splendor!

The younger brother tried to hide his fear, but seeing his friend turn into a snake made him terrified. That night he was so afraid that he could not eat or sleep.

Finally, he went to see his older brother. "What is wrong with you? Are you sick?" the older brother asked.

"No, I am not sick, but I feel afraid and troubled." Then the boy told his older brother what had happened.

"Are you so afraid of the naga that you do not want to see your friend anymore?" asked the older brother. "Yes," replied the younger boy. For a while neither spoke. Finally the older brother said, "Then do as I say. On his head the naga has a precious gem that gives him magical powers. Tomorrow, ask him to give you his jewel. Ask him the same thing each day for three days."

The next day the boy did as his brother had advised and asked the naga for his jewel. Although the naga loved his friend very much, he could not part with the precious stone, the source of his power, beauty, and magic. The following day the boy asked the same thing. Also on the third day he repeated, "Please, give me your jewel."

The serpent-king grew very sad and thought, "All my friend wants from me is my jewel. He does not love me anymore." Sighing deeply, he went back to his palace under the river Ganges and did not return to the younger brother's hut.

Alone in his hut, day after day, the boy began to miss his companion. He thought about the naga and his magical jewel so much that soon he could think of nothing else. He dreamed of the jewel day and night, and could not eat, drink, or sleep. He even forgot to visit his brother to tell him what had happened.

Soon the older brother became concerned and came down to the river's bank to see if his brother was all right. He was shocked to see him so pale and thin. "What is the matter with you, little brother?"

"I never see my friend anymore," the boy replied. "I really miss him, but I also wish I had his beautiful magical jewel."

The older brother smiled and said, "The naga will never give you his jewel unless you show him that you care more for him than for the stone. Asking him for the jewel has driven your friend away. Perhaps if you love him as he loves you, he will want to share his jewel with you." After having said this, the older brother went away.

The boy thought of his friend and the good times they had shared. Maybe what his older brother said was true. He walked down to the river and called, "Friend! Friend! Please come out!"

The serpent-king heard the boy's voice and raised his head out of the water. Looking deep into the naga's eyes, the younger brother's fear completely vanished. Seeing this, the naga smiled and came up onto the river bank.

Sitting next to the boy, the naga gently shook his head, allowing the precious stone to fall from his crown. It fell right at the boy's feet. In wonder he picked up the shining jewel and began to play with it. At sunset, when it was time for the serpent-king to return to his palace in the river, the younger brother gently put the jewel back on the naga's head and said, "Good night, my friend!"

"Good night," the naga responded, and then vanished into the darkness. For the rest of their lives the serpent-king and the younger brother who lived on the bank of the great river Ganges shared their friendship like a jewel. Nourished by respect and understanding, their friendship became more precious and magical than any jewel could be.

My page

Colored by _____

PARENTS AND TEACHERS CORNER

The Jataka Tales nurture in readers young and old an appreciation for values shared by all the world's great spiritual traditions. Read aloud, performed and studied for centuries, they communicate universal values such as kindness, forgiveness, compassion, humility, courage, honesty and patience. You can bring this story alive through the suggestions on these pages. Actively engaging with the stories creates a bridge to the children in your life and opens a dialogue about what brings joy, stability and caring.

The Jewel Of Friendship

In *The Jewel of Friendship* a young man befriends a naga, a powerful serpent-king who disguises himself as a human being. When the boy discovers the naga's true identity, he is frightened. His older brother wishes to help him overcome his fear and advises him to ask the serpent-king for the jewel that is the source of the naga's power, beauty and magic. This greediness saddens the naga and he ends their friendship. The boy then realizes that the jewel of friendship is far more precious than any ordinary gem and their friendship is deepened.

Key Values
Generosity
Friendship

Bringing the story to life

Asking the children questions about the events and values in the story will deepen their understanding and enrich their vocabulary. For example:

- Why is the boy happy to have a friend?
- What would happen if the serpent-king gave his jewel away?
- Why is the naga disappointed?
- Have you ever had a special friend?
- Is friendship important in your life and why?

To explore the story further have the children act out an everyday example of fear and greediness. Then assign each child roles such as the elder or younger brother, and let them play out the situation as they imagine the characters would.

Discussion topics and questions can be modified depending on the age of the child.

Learning through play

Children enjoy trying out new ideas, using all five senses to make discoveries. Use the story to encourage their creativity:

- Have the children color in or draw a scene or character that intrigues them. Then invite them to talk about what it means to them, exploring the key values.
- Make masks for all the characters.
- Paint the masks and decorate them.
- Let each child choose a character to impersonate. Imitate the voices, and bring the two brothers and the naga to life. Then switch roles.
- Display the key values somewhere visible and refer to them regularly during the day.
- Make up your own story with them.

Active reading

- Even before children can read, they enjoy storybooks and love growing familiar with the characters and drawings. You can show them the pictures in this book and tell the story in your own words.
- By going over the book with the children two or three times and helping them to recognize words you help them to build vocabulary.
- Children love to hear the same story with different and sometimes exaggerated voices for each character.
- Integrate the wisdom of the story into everyday life. When tempers flare or patience is called for, remind the child of what the younger brother went through.
- Carry a book whenever you leave the house in case you have some unexpected time to go back to the story.
- Talk about the story while you and the children are engaged in daily activities like washing the dishes or driving to school.

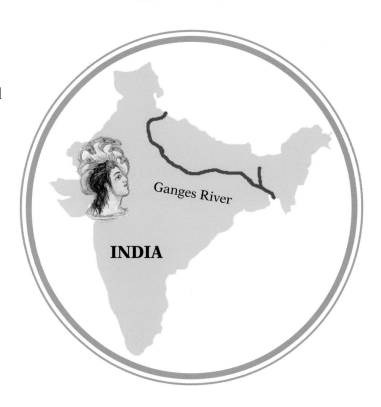

Names and places

India: The source of many spiritual traditions and the background of most of the Jatakas (accounts of the Buddha's previous lives). People seeking wisdom have always viewed India's forests and jungles as favorable places for solitary retreats. The Buddha taught the Jatakas to clarify the workings of karma, the relationship between actions and results.

River Ganges: Winding 1,500 miles across northern India, this great river is revered as a goddess and plays a role in numerous myths.

Benares: A holy city in North central India, on the river Ganges. One of the most ancient cities in the world, it is also known as Varanasi.

Naga: In Indian mythology: serpent like creatures who live under water. Nature spirits and protectors of springs and rivers that have a profound influence on the environment.

The Jataka Tales are folk tales that were transmitted orally, memorized and passed from generation to generation for hundreds of years. We are grateful for the opportunity to offer them to you. May they inspire fresh insight into the dynamics of human relationships and may understanding grow with each reading.

The Jataka Tales are for children aged three to eight

JATAKA TALES SERIES

The Jewel of Friendship

A story about an unusual friendship

A boy befriends a naga, disguised as a young man of about the same age. When the naga reveals his true snake-like form, the boy rejects him out of fear. Only when he misses his special companion, does he learn the meaning of friendship.

$8.95 in USA
ISBN 13: 978-0-89800-428-1

9 780898 004281

50895 >

REGENTS HIGH SCHOOL

MATHEMATICS

B

Parts II, III and IV

WestSea Publishing Co. Inc.

Exam Review Workbook

[Student Constructed Response Questions]